The Case of Jake's Escape

Written by
Laura Appleton-Smith

Illustrated by
Carol Vredenburgh

Laura Appleton-Smith holds a degree in English from Middlebury College.
Laura is a primary schoolteacher who has combined her talents in creative writing with
her experience in early childhood education to create *Books to Remember*.
She lives in New Hampshire with her husband Terry.

Carol Vredenburgh graduated Summa Cum Laude from Syracuse University and has worked
as an artist and illustrator ever since. This is the sixth book she has illustrated for Flyleaf Publishing.

A Book to Remember™
Published by Flyleaf Publishing
Post Office Box 287, Lyme, NH 03768

For orders or information, contact us at **(800) 449-7006**.
Please visit our website at **www.flyleafpublishing.com**

First Edition
Library of Congress Catalog Card Number: 2005935763
Hard cover ISBN-13: 978-1-929262-45-8
Hard cover ISBN-10: 1-929262-45-0
Soft cover ISBN-13: 978-1-929262-46-5
Soft cover ISBN-10: 1-929262-46-9

For our beloved Jake.

LAS

—

For Cocoa.

CV

Chapter 1: D and D's Detective Desk

In the summer Dan and Dave run "D and D's Detective Desk".

The fact is that Dan and Dave are first-rate
at getting things back that are lost.

They found Jon's pet snake in the cabinet under the sink.

They found Abe's lost button under the drapes.

They even found Mrs. Crane's jade locket hidden in the grass at the baseball game.

Chapter 2: D and D's Next Case

One day Dan and Dave were inspecting insects with their detective glasses when Mrs. Crane came running down the lane.

"Dan and Dave, my dog Jake has escaped!
Can you help to get him back?" Mrs. Crane asked
as she felt the jade locket on her neck.

"When did Jake escape?" Dan asked.

"I left at ten o'clock to get coconut flakes and apricot jam. I was running a bit late and in my haste I made a mistake and did not lock the gate," Mrs. Crane told him.

"Do not panic Mrs. Crane, D and D are on the case,"
Dan said as he got dressed to hunt for Jake.

"Mrs. Crane, one last thing…Can you tell us
Jake's favorite places to visit?" Dave asked.

"The lake, the baseball field, the skating rink...and the bank where Jake gets dog snacks from the bank teller named Kate," she told him.

Dan and Dave went to the lake.

They waded out to the swim instructor and asked,

"Have you spotted a lost Great Dane named Jake?"

"Yes," the instructor told them, "we were in the middle of
a race when all of a sudden a BIG dog jumped into the lake.
He swam so fast he won the race!"

"Is he still at the lake?" Dave asked.

"No, he ran off dripping wet. He went to the skating rink,"
the swim instructor told them.

When Dan and Dave got to the rink a skater was yelling,
"The puck, the puck! That BIG dog made off with the puck!"

Dan and Dave asked a skater what happened.

"A BIG wet dog just ran into the middle of the face-off.
He picked up the puck and ran out that exit!" the skater told them.

Out the exit, Dave and Dan spotted
Jake's wet tracks on the pavement.

He had run to the baseball game.

At the game the fans were yelling and jumping up and down.

"What happened?" Dan and Dave asked the ump.

"The batter made a base hit when all of a sudden…

A BIG dog ran into the game. He grabbed the baseball and ran out that gate, but he did drop this puck at home plate," the ump told them.

Dan and Dave ran out the gate. There were six men with rakes and spades standing next to a block of wet pavement.

"Has a lost Great Dane run past?" they asked.

"You bet," a man told them, "that BIG dog ran smack-dab into the middle of this wet pavement. He zigzagged in and out of the rakes and spades as if he was in a maze."

Jake's tracks went into a tent in front of Jane's dress shop.

Under the tent were racks of dresses and hats and jackets on sale.

Dave and Dan spotted Jake. He was running under the racks.
He was draped with a dress and had a hat strapped on his neck.

"Stop that Great Dane!" they yelled.

Jake ran into the bank with Dan and Dave hot on his tracks.
When Dan and Dave got to him, Jake was sitting next to
Kate's desk. He was dressed in a red spotted dress and a pink hat.
A baseball sat on the rug next to him.

"Jake has been lost all day, but we found him at last!"
Dave told Kate, "Now we can bring him back to Mrs. Crane."

"I will go with you," Kate said, "it is the end of my day
at the bank."

So off they went, but first they stopped at Jane's tent sale
to drop off the dress and the hat. When they told Jane Jake's tale,
she wanted to visit Mrs. Crane too.

On their way to drop the baseball back at the game
the paving men were just packing up. They were so glad
that Jake was found, they made their way with the gang
to Mrs. Crane's.

At the baseball field the game had ended.
The ump still had the puck, so he went with the gang
to drop it off at the rink.

When they dropped off the puck, the gang picked up several skaters; and at the lake they picked up several swimmers. What a fan club Jake had!

Mrs. Crane was so glad that Jake was safe.

"Dan and Dave, you are first rate at getting things back that are lost!" Mrs. Crane said as she hugged Jake's neck.

"We could not have cracked the case without the help of Jake's fan club!" Dave told her as he waved to the gang.

"I just baked a cake," Mrs. Crane told them, "let's have it to celebrate."

So Mrs. Crane cut the cake and put it on plates.

It was a vanilla cake with apricot filling and coconut flake frosting.

And it tasted great...

Even to a BIG Great Dane named Jake!

The Case of Jake's Escape is decodable with the 26 phonetic alphabet sounds plus the "a_e" phonogram, and the ability to blend those sounds together.

Puzzle Words are words used in the story that are either irregular or may have sound/spelling correspondences that the reader may not be familiar with.

The **Puzzle Word Review List** contains Puzzle Words that have been introduced in previous books in the *Books to Remember* Series.

Please Note: If all of the words on this page are pre-taught and the reader knows the 26 phonetic alphabet sounds, plus the phonogram listed above, and has the ability to blend those sounds together, this book is 100% phonetically decodable.

Puzzle Words:

- chapter
- coconut
- detective
- favorite
- field
- first
- found
- great
- home
- instructor
- middle
- shop
- vanilla
- way

Puzzle Word Review List:

a	onto
all	out
are	put
as	said
ball	she
been	so
could	that
day	the
do	their
down	them
even	then
for	there
from	they
front	this
go	to
has	told
have	too
he	visit
her	wanted
his	was
I	we
into	were
is	what
Mrs.	when
my	where
no	with
o'clock	without
of	you
one	

"a_e" words:

Abe's	Kate's
baked	lake
base	lane
baseball	late
cake	made
came	maze
case	mistake
celebrate	named
Crane	pavement
Crane's	places
Dane	plate
Dave	plates
draped	race
drapes	rakes
escape	rate
escaped	safe
face	sale
flakes	skaters
game	snake
gate	spades
haste	tale
jade	tasted
Jake	waded
Jake's	waved
Jane's	
Kate	paving
	skating

"ed" words:	**"ing" words:**
ask**ed**	gett**ing**
bak**ed**	th**ing**
crack**ed**	th**ing**s
drap**ed**	br**ing**
dress**ed**	dripp**ing**
dropp**ed**	fill**ing**
end**ed**	frost**ing**
escap**ed**	inspect**ing**
grabb**ed**	jump**ing**
happen**ed**	pack**ing**
hugg**ed**	pav**ing**
jump**ed**	runn**ing**
nam**ed**	sitt**ing**
peddl**ed**	skat**ing**
pick**ed**	stand**ing**
spott**ed**	yell**ing**
stopp**ed**	
strapp**ed**	
tast**ed**	**"er" words:**
wad**ed**	
want**ed**	batt**er**
wav**ed**	skat**er**
yell**ed**	skat**er**s
zigzagg**ed**	summ**er**
	swimm**er**s
	tell**er**
	und**er**